SIDEBROW BOOKS

H & G

Published by Sidebrow Books
P.O. Box 86921
Portland, OR 97286
sidebrow@sidebrow.net
www.sidebrow.net

Cover art by Hong Seon Jang
"Black Forest" (tape on chalkboard)
courtesy of David B. Smith Gallery
Cover & book design by Jason Snyder

ISBN: 1-940090-08-3
ISBN-13: 978-1-940090-08-5

FIRST EDITION | FIRST PRINTING
9 8 7 6 5 4 3 2 1
SIDEBROW BOOKS 019
PRINTED IN THE UNITED STATES

Sidebrow Books titles are distributed by
Small Press Distribution

Titles are available directly from Sidebrow at
www.sidebrow.net/books

Sidebrow is a member of the Intersection Incubator, a program of Intersection for the Arts (www.theintersection.org) providing fiscal sponsorship, incubation, and consulting for artists. Contributions to Sidebrow are tax-deductible to the extent allowed by law.

H & G

ANNA MARIA HONG

SIDEBROW BOOKS • 2018 • PORTLAND & SAN FRANCISCO

"I always believe stories whilst they are being told," said the Cockroach.

"You are a wise creature," said the Old Woman. "That is what stories are for."

—"The Story of the Eldest Princess" by A.S. Byatt

I

The Sticky Stuff

The candy gets on the inside because we eat it and eat it like thieves, like children under a great burr of clouds made by a god in a slothful mood.

The candy gets on the outside and sticks like tragedy, marking us as the worst type of person. It sticks like the worst time.

What was the worst time? We can't remember it, but we can feel it like a smear of embers inside our small chests.

The worst time was when G. had to push the Witch.

The worst time was when Father left us in the Woods with nothing but crumbs and stones.

The worst time was when he did it again, and we knew he was lying.

The worst time was when Mother died and everything after that.

We remember everything of course. We're broken, not naïve.

We remember the sharp wind moving the yellow leaves across the Woods, as we walked on and on looking for nothing, though we were very hungry and cold and felt a new bad feeling, a sticky burning that kept us moving. Then we ate the candy and could not stop eating.

The worst time was when the Witch gripped H.'s hand and told him to stop eating.

The worst time was hearing the Witch screaming, though she had wanted to kill us and eat us.

Other things stick to the candy such as the adults' remarks about our greediness and astonishing cruelty. We should be more forgiving like normal children, they say. Those remarks stick because we don't know who they belong to—them or us—and sometimes we don't know if the words are on the outside or not.

of the Believer who made the world by believing in it. If the Believer stopped believing, would the world cease to exist? H. thinks it wiser to not risk it, so he prays every day, climbing the green and brown peaks, dirt and gravel slipping under his well-worn feet, until he reaches the New Witch's hut where he will suck on the Witch's cold tits, ripe and smooth as the flesh of pale green fruit. They taste like cold soup, and each day H. will climb the mountain to suck first one Witch's tit then another, sucking each globe until it is dry and wrinkled like a fava bean, like the face of the Witch, a face that has seen the beginning of this world and a face and fucking mind that had once tried to eat him.

H. had loved that Witch's house, devouring each translucent red window pane with his eyes and mouth, each succulent door handle and decorative sugar knob, as the fat, greedy boy that he was—chubby, pale, good for nothing but being consumed in a human-flavored tartare or roast one might serve to a passive Father who had married badly after being widowed, marrying a woman with small hips and red lips in a hard face with a will of gold glittering like malice beneath her unlined skin. But that was a world ago; H.'s Stepmother was long dead, mysteriously, suddenly dead upon H. & G.'s return to the cottage where, as far as H. knows, their Father still lives.

Of G., H. knows even less. He remembers her packing a small red box one day when they were ten years old and disappearing with it into the black-leaved forest over the snow-covered mountain. H. thought that she might come back, but she did not, and after the first century or so, H. was no longer surprised. G. had never really trusted their Father after the first abandonment, and more to the point, G. had had no need of him, which had become clear to H. when she'd shoved the Witch into the oven.

H. remembers the startling decisiveness of his sister's action, watching her push the crone into the enormous oven from his seat in the corner, his face covered with sugar, his hand in a cloudberry pie. He remembers crying, "No!" and G. telling him to shut up as she slammed the hot iron door shut and pressed against it with both arms and all her might. He remembers the Witch's curses and cries as she kicked the oven from the inside and, of course, the horrid smell of her burning flesh.

Usually ravening, H. would not eat for weeks after that, not during the whole long walk home to their Father's cottage, which seemed to take weeks, not days, and not for many days after that. He remembers their Father raising a worried brow upon seeing him and asking, "Why is Hansel so skinny?" which G. answered wordlessly with a look of rage that never subsided when their Father was around.

H. knows now as he did not know then that G. was always on the verge of leaving, of abandoning him like a trail of crumbs or their dead Mother or once ferocious, now dead Stepmother. Sometimes he thinks about the red box when he is sucking on the New Witch's tits, which he loves to think about whether he is sucking on them or not.

He thinks of them in his hands when he is walking up the steep hill alone each day, how he will take one in both hands, pinching and licking the surprisingly large wine-colored nipple until the tit is sucked dry and flat as a poor man's wallet. How he will move on to the next one once the first one is done and suck that one too until it is spent, and the New Witch cries out her terrifying cry and pushes his head away, and the Believer grants the world another day.

The Believer believes in sexual ritual.

The Believer has made gods castrate each other to birth love in her fickleness and beauty.

H. understands that every day is a prayer as seduction, supplication as taking and not giving anything back but pleasure, which is incidental to the giver. H. sucks like his life depends on it, because it is what he is good at—the only thing he has always been good at—eating, siphoning dominion and beauty from powerful women who want to save him and eat him.

The Witch strokes his golden hair as she suckles him, telling him how good he has been, how sturdy he is, how well he climbed the mountain, how good he is to save the world like this, how strong and authoritative his hands are on her cold, ripe, deceptively youthful body. H. feels he can do anything when he is drinking and holding the Witch's tits, which grow a little warmer as he sucks them, softer around the dark diamond-hard nipple, softer and warmer until each tit is spent, H.'s task for the day done.

Afterward, the Witch's face is restored to youth, smooth as a plum, though her body is as flat and shriveled as a hag's. H. is frequently exhausted afterward, though he feels competent and satisfied with his work.

He prefers the Witch the other way around, the way she looks at him when he first enters her hut, with her ancient visage, spotted and overtanned—burnt too many times in the high-altitude sun—with her clear brown eyes, not unkind. Unbuttoning a tight semi-transparent shirt or letting him unbutton it to reveal one full, hanging Witch's tit, new each time in H.'s mouth.

The Witch is thousands of years old, as is H. though H. has retained all the strength and lubriciousness of youth through some strange genetic or geographical miracle. They are the only two beings in this village at the edge of the world, and they may be the only two in this whole world, thinks H. "I'm lucky she has nice tits," he says to no one in particular. "It could be worse. I could have no skills at all."

Someday the New Witch will tire of me too—prayer and fate of the world be damned—or she will die and either way I'll be abandoned again, surmises H. Alone with nothing but this rocky, dirty peak to climb, an empty hut at the top.

Was it Freud who said,

"Everything in the world is about sex except sex. Sex is about power," or some other canny adult male who knew something about the practice of sex as power, knew it as observer, abettor, or serial perpetrator.

The difference between the pervert and the moral human is self-pity. The moral human can at some point say, "I did it. I did those disgusting things." The pervert exerts his power through complaint fueled by a bottomless belief in his victimization, the irreparable injustices done to him or her by a society that never got him.

The pervert—more than the victims and more than any ordinary woman or man—needs to believe that he is a good person, an immaculate person who has never done harm to anyone. She is crushed and surprised by the anger of her victims from whom she expects gratitude as well as acquiescence.

All the facts have escaped the pervert from the beginning:

i. The fact that the child will inevitably grow up to be an adult surpassing him in strength and ability.

ii. The fact that there is no statute of limitation on revenge.

iii. The fact that the pervert will be an old man someday, no longer valued in the world for his prowess, his extraordinary gifts.

The pervert will not see that power, that ineluctable sweet, has congealed, sealing her in. After years of self-blame for being in the wrong place at the right time, the grown child will replace the golden mirror with an ordinary glass, holding it up for all the world to see.

G. IS WALKING UP THE HILL

with her alert mind and ordinary breasts, which are neither large nor magically self-renewing. Having no particular destination in mind and no home to go back to, having divested herself of her few possessions, and having trained all desires but the most monstrously immediate out of herself over three decades, not through some philosophical determination to be good but rather through an overriding desire to not feel any more disappointment, that candy house of pain with its ever regenerating shoots of twisted gingerbread and spice: her Father/Stepmother packing her and her brother off into the wild Woods, Stepmother's hard, hypocritical smile, which only an idiot like their Father would fall for again and again, G. walks and recalls the axe in the tree rigged explicitly to fool them into continuing on by themselves deeper into the Enchanted Woods and the fact that they found the sound of an axe comforting.

When G. thinks of H., she refers to them as "we," embracing the booby prize of language for real experience. She knows that she can say *we, we, we* all she wants, but the fact remains that it's her and just her, because H. was helpless the second he crossed the threshold of the Witch's house and equally helpless in the face of their Father's betrayal. H. could never see that, at the very least, their Father had agreed to cast them out to be eaten by wolves or bears or a Witch. H. could never get mad at their Father; he blamed it all on their dead Stepmother, conveniently dead upon their arrival back at the cottage.

For a while, G. too had thought it could be alright, as their Father had promised to never lie to them again. But within a year he had remarried, as he was a man who could not live without a wife. G. remembers her Father, the Woodsman, struggling to open a can of potted meat, and she remembers impatiently doing it for him, disgusted and knowing then that it would just be a matter of time before he found a second replacement for their Mother.

The third wife was younger than the others, still slightly plump with youthful excess and soon pregnant with their half-brother. As far as G. knew, their new Stepmother never proposed expelling H. and herself from the cottage, but then they had learned to need so little, gratefully eating the bland root soup she made nearly every night, grateful for the straw beds, the roof made of slate, the walls made of stone, the door made of pine. The windows, of course, were made of glass. G. tested them daily, licking each pane to make sure it hadn't turned into sugar. She would have rapped them out, if she'd had the nerve, which she did not.

As it was, she simply didn't last long in that solid house. Like the other wives, their new Stepmother had full sway over their Father, and she did not like H. and G. To all appearances, the new Stepmother was competent and neutral, and particularly attentive when they were ill. Who knows why, but H. was ecstatic when she put a cool cloth on his forehead and fed him broth made from chicken bones and peas. G. was very rarely sick and not so easy to help even then—especially then, so great was her hunger, equal to her enormous distrust of all persons charged with her and her brother's well being.

So impoverished was her ability to overcome these obstacles, which after an age, she could perceive and feel as heavy stones in her pockets. Try as she might, she could not cast those stones out upon the forest floor. Those, she instead took across the Sea with her through all her wanderings.

Dream Song 218 / G.

"Most women," said the older, shaggy haired man with graying curls, "don't have style, but *you*," he paused to look directly at G., "you are beautiful, and I hope I always feel this way."

G. found this statement disturbing, coming from a man she thought was her mentor. It was like being told she was attractive by a male therapist after telling him the whole sordid story of abandonment, narrowly avoided cannibalism, and her brother's helplessness, and this mentor's statement instantly turned the dinner into a weird date. Had she been so naïve again? How was this possible for someone like her, a survivor if there ever was one and someone who had had the luxury of cluelessness regarding caretakers' intentions stripped away long, long ago?

She did not like the emphasis on her physical person in this context, and she especially did not like the privileging of *his* assessment of her outward style above any of her opinions. The therapist had been real—a couple's counselor she had seen with her ex-boyfriend in her twenties—but this smiling man with the gray curls, an established writer who had taken her under his golden wing, was simulacrum like the dreamt-into-being gods of fire and mud in a modern tale. He was a figure of her own invention—a messenger from her own mind—so what, if anything, was he trying to convey? This old-school control King, this benevolent, pernicious, sexist lech embedded in her own recesses, her own will?

He was a man known for his wit. And this was a reminder, a joke about her rapacious, usury attitude toward her "style," which depended partly on being different from other women, women who hadn't had to kill the Witch, women and men who never had to choose between their own lives and someone else's. G. had defended herself and saved her bewildered brother, but often, it still didn't feel that way. Often, she felt like she had no hands to hold fast the door and keep the Witch in. Too often, the Witch with her gray curls would rise again in different guise like a Wolf in well-meaning skin.

Have I trammeled the fields of gold?
§ I have died and died and died

Just as one can never be sure that one hasn't died, one can never be quite sure that one has died and gone to H_______. "If this is the life of the mind, then I am dead," thinks G. "For all of Paradise, my life was simply not worth living."

Regretting nothing, G. has very little to show for her fervor, her perseverance, her sporting cheer. Ha ha ha.

Ha ha ha ha. Ha. Ha. Ha. Ha.

She has seen the petulant rewarded with care and acceptance. She has felt burning envy for that bland state contingent upon a blankness she cannot muster.

Once you shove a Witch into an oven; once you've been shoved into the Woods with the Witch, a helpless charge, the Father/Woodsman's axe swinging from a tree, and a handful of crumbs; once you've heard your brother tell you, "She's nice, she feeds me, what's your problem?" while you've grown weak and thin; once you've been underestimated not once, not twice, but three times in the same goddamned Woods and once you decide to leave all that BEHIND for ill, for better or worse, blankness is simply not an option.

H. hated G. for telling him to stop eating unless he wanted to be eaten, and saving him had made no difference. He blamed G. for the psychic scars, the memory of the burning Witch, and for leaving an unbearable situation. They all blamed G. because she was the weakest and the fiercest and because G. hated them back, unlike H. who doesn't hate anyone.

No one likes the girl-hero in this story, except for the girl outside the story, the girl holding the picture book at recess, sitting under an oak tree on a stone step. The girl has already heard this story many times; it was read to her when she was learning to read, following the flight of black letters around the pictures and colors. She will read the story again and again, perfectly content under that tree. She knows something herself about abandonment, but nothing like what is to come, as she herself grows older, wiser, stranger, and thus more vulnerable.

Ode to my love that you might know my power
—by the New Witch

Ode to the smell of Hansel in the morning—
Ode to the saint of perpetual ascension—
    My love, with the missing incisor.
    My love, his chest a plank of wood.
        My love, with legs straight as wool on fire.

My love, with eyes like blue famine.
        My love, whose lips are full like September.
My love, whose lips are a berry infantada
    & activity & unhappiness &

    red shutters like the minds of old men.

Gretel as bad temper incarnate.

Three kinds of desire

(1) "Tell me I'm *the* fairest, tell me I'm your number one," said the Witch to H. "Tell me this, and I will leave you alone," she entreated, embarrassed by this most unoccult request, but after four or five whiskeys the plea came out. After centuries of power, she was still bad at holding her liquor.

H. looked concerned, a look that instantly devastated and enraged the Witch. "Well, I, well, I, well, I," said H.

"Forget it," said the Witch.

Later that night, alone in her chambers, the Witch gazed at her small black mirror and tried to write, "You are a coward," over and over, but she was too far gone to write legibly.

(2) "More pie, please," said H., mouth full of cream. He held his knife with the left hand, the fork in his right, very precisely, self-consciously, as if he had been trained at an advanced but still impressionable age.

(3) Even in middle age, G. missed having a Mother. She had not had a parent who needed less than she did. Her Father and Stepmother had been traumatized by the wars that had ravaged the Enchanted Woods when they were growing up, and both had lost their Mothers in childhood. Like her own

biological Mother, G.'s Stepmother's Mother had died in labor, giving birth in an alpine field alone with only the rotting apples and ants for company.

Her Father's Mother had died when he was nine. A beauty with long black hair, unhappily married to G.'s Grandfather, a mountain farmer who cared more about the vagaries of his crops than his wife and son. G.'s Grandmother sat outside their cottage reading storybooks to her adoring child, smoking cigarettes, and drinking cherry wine until she died her untimely death, abandoning her son who never forgave her or his Father.

A GORGEOUS RAINY DAY . . .

I make these ugly marks on the calendar, a slash through another day lived. Why do it? But then, as the saying goes, why do anything?

Why not make something ugly or beautiful; it's a gorgeous rainy day, misting, and there are thousands of shades of gray, my favorite color, out there through my window.

October is a hunched bird with a small head, black lips around a red egg. The egg, the lips, the tiny head made of cells the shape of feathers.

I died in just this way: as an egg with no shell, swallowed by lips the color of Spanish slugs, the color of rancid honey, wrapped in a thousand decisive strokes.

I died the way I was born: first me, pop! and then another.

The water today is a beautiful gray-dark green like malachite morning ripple by wave, like the sound of sugar in the Witch's throat.

I did not hate her.

Unlike the others, she had the decency to be straight with us.

"I'd like to eat you," she said. "As soon as that boy is as plump as a *to-mah-to*."

Maybe I did hate her. Even at the age of eight, I'd found assumed accents extremely irritating. And where did she learn such pretensions, living alone, blind from cataracts, in those desolate woods with nothing better to do than to build that delectable house. How long did she labor?

"Seven years," she said. "Seven years of daily conjuring—willing this *luhhr* into being."

—milky caramel

—hard peppermint—

shiny black chocolate—

—vanilla crème—

violet gumdrops—

marzipan fruit—

I would have felt sorry for her if she hadn't been so grotesque, so hard to look at and so full of justified outrage, complaining about everything from the weather to a neighbor cutting down a tree between their houses.

"Too much sun now!" she declared. "It will melt my windows!"

The windows were a marvel: intricate, brightly colored, hard-candy panes set like the rose windows in Gothic cathedrals.

The Witch often bemoaned our nation's ongoing war with X_______, a small oil-rich country across the Sea. We had been an oil-rich country once, but by the time H. and I were born, the oil and most of the people had gone. Food and heat were in short supply throughout the Enchanted Woods. "They've been bombing those innocent people for decades. We've never stopped bombing them," she would say, looking up from the daily paper.

Like I said, her grievances were mostly justified, and they were deployed in a steady rotation. She grumbled, of course, about the constant drizzle, like all the other adults. The injustice that seemed to rankle her the most though was the fact that the locals had never warmed to her. She had lived in the Enchanted Woods for twelve years, attending municipal meetings, contributing opinion pieces to the newspaper, giving money to the Women's Craft Council, and donating her own esteemed sculptures to the town. She had been a model citizen, and she was the only craftsperson in the Woods whose work was nationally known.

"I cannot tell you how many times I've met people in this town for a perfectly pleasant cup of coffee, and that's the end of it," she would begin.

At that time, I had lived in the Woods all my young life, so I would just nod or say something like, "We go to sleep early here. Most adults don't leave their houses much."

Such niceties would assuage the Witch for a little while, but inevitably I would burn a pie or let the soup boil over or fail in one of the many other domestic duties I had been charged with. By the time I pushed her into the oven, I was doing all the cooking, cleaning, and yard work, so that the Witch could be free to concentrate on what she called her real work: building another candy house like the one that H. and I had set upon and been entrapped by.

She had a studio lined with cedar, cork, and candy canes in the back of the house, and in that studio she was building a tiny model of her new child trap. Almost finished, it looked exactly like the one we lived in. Every now and then, or rather, every day at noon, she would emerge from the studio screaming.

"Aaaaarrrrrgh!"

"What?" I said the first time it happened. "Is it the rain again? The Fowler says it's supposed to be sunny by mid-afternoon."

"No!" said the Witch. "And I don't care what the Fowler says. It's this damn project. I feel like I'm not learning anything new; it's all old familiar turf. I'm bored with it, and it's not coming together."

"Oh," I said. "Why do you do it?"

"Because I have to," said the Witch distractedly, bony fingers running through her supernaturally blonde hair. She stared at me with her pale eyes and added, "You would like for me to abandon the project, wouldn't you? The way you were abandoned by your pathetic parents. I'm going to build that house, and as soon as I do, I'm going to eat your brother, *scrahhwny* or not. And don't think you'll be the last children I consume."

She stormed back into the studio, where I could hear her listening to the news on the radio and talking to her cats, Vie and Die, fraternal twins like me and H. I went back to scrubbing the cauldrons, which hadn't been cleaned in years.

By the time I shoved her into the spotless oven, I'd heard everything about the Witch's life at least three times or at least everything that she remembered at the advanced age she was—42? 109? Or everything dramatic enough to tell.

How her parents would beat her mercilessly if she failed to make the floors shine like mirrors or if she got a bad grade. How she had excelled at the Burgher's College, mastering both the arts and sciences. How her best friend had lost an arm in a terrible lab fire. How she had been the only woman admitted to the Institute of Culinary Rheology and Design, which she had dropped out of after a year, so severe was the sexual harassment. How her younger sister, often mistaken for the glamorous Queen of E________, had died long ago after being committed to a cottage for the insane.

Apparently, the Witch too had been attractive, though as I said, by the time H. and I met her, she was difficult to look at: terribly thin from a strict diet—most of the food I made was thrown out—and though her skin was smooth, it was covered in spots, which she attributed to having taken a magical pill repeatedly to please an old boyfriend whose preferences I also learned too much about during that interminable period, which seemed like years, but in reality had lasted only a few weeks, seven to be exact, which seems incredible to me now, but perhaps tells you something about the nature of enchantment.

You may also have noticed that the Witch had neighbors, right next door—close enough to cut down her favorite tree. H. and I could have run to those neighbors for help at any time during our imprisonment, but we did not, despite knowing all too well that the Witch wanted to kill us and eat us.

But you have to remember a few things:

(1) This was an enchanted house, enchanted not in the least by the fact that at least one of us was being fed and fed very well, first by the Witch herself, an especially good pastry chef, and then by me, then as ever a quick study.

(2) We had arrived starving and abandoned not once but twice by our beloved Father and innocuous seeming Stepmother. Though cruel, the Witch was direct about her intentions, and the neighbors would very likely have returned us to our original abandoners, who would have very likely turned us out again.

(3) I, for one, was not totally convinced that the Witch would kill us. She seemed to be enjoying complaining and threatening and yelling at us so much, and she was so easily fooled by the chicken bone I held out each night in lieu of H.'s arm. "Haaaach!" she'd hiss like her cat Vie. "Still so skinny!"

I kept the house in order while she raged about and pretended to work. She had someone to tell her worst stories to: dumb kids she was going to eat, two helpless rejects who had been wandering homeless in the Woods. No one could have been a better ear, and those embarrassing secrets would be safe, sailing with us to the grave or staying within the candy house's four walls. Or so she must have thought in that sharp, deluded mind—sharpened and beclouded by decades of experience that reaffirmed her preset notions, as experience tends to do.

I shoved her into that oven because I instinctively knew that it would be the end to something that I had already felt working its way around me like a fog or a cloud of smoke, a pattern, in the old parlance. I killed her because I didn't want to hear another heroic or awful story from those vehement lips, another woe—rational or ludicrous—from this person who could not break the habit of malice in spite of her extraordinary powers. This person who could have been my hero and our savior but who was instead another cautionary tale—another sad fate to avoid.

Baked Witch

G. had gotten what she let herself want:

a roof over her head,

a warm place to sleep,

nice but irritating cottagemates too wrapped up in their own problems
to bother much with her well- or ill-being

No time to talk about your feelings, G. So your parents abandoned you and the Witch tried to eat you, and your brother was and remains useless. They don't miss you; they're better off without you, but they let you feel like you were the bad one, leaving. They only ever wanted H., the good one, the fat one, the boy. Try to be nicer to everyone you meet. Chop some wood for the Woodsman, shoot some birds for the Fowler, shoot something else for the Huntsman. They have children. They're too busy.

When you get tired of holding up the culture—you and your loserly single friends—you can go back to your hole, which is what you can afford, since you spent all that time making things other than bread, meat, and silver. What exactly were you doing?

Fixing yourself?

Getting "clean"?

You never were the grateful type. Biting all those hands that fed you.

G.'s rebuttal: Well.

Well, the rhetoric of hate remains alive and well within me and without. I'm certainly not the only person in or out of the Enchanted Woods who feels this way, no matter how bewildered you act. I've taken great care to spare future victims by not marrying, not having children, and not telling people what complete fucking idiots they are. But I believe you.

I am so disgusting, so intrinsically repulsive. You are correct: No one wants a woman who walks away from misery. And all my stories are fading away from me anyway—I can barely remember what or where I was last month, and if that horror is lodged in my ugly, broken body—in my shoulder, my neck, my aching foot, so be it. I can't fix this. With all my heart and all my naiveté and all my wood and all my mind. Like a bad apple, that poison's here to stay.

There's no fix for my loserliness, but there is an endless supply of it as long as I may live. Like my own nurse, all I can do is adjust the pillows and make myself a little more comfortable in this terminal lameness, administering the equivalent of a morphine drip, which would be this:

sex
aggression
writing
music
dance
art
acupuncture
movies
travel
feng shui
massage
chatting
chanting
running
swimming
yoga
astrology
the great and terrible stories

II

I BELIEVE THAT THOSE OF YOU

who aren't repulsive should be helping those of us who are. It's only fair. That would be justice.

As gray as dysgraphia

October's an iron pot full of small golden birds, boiling and singing like flames. Their quartet of throats is an echo, a chamber of doves and wild men tearing out fistfuls of beard. All of this menace at the back of my throat itching like a populace, singing like a note, like a state of inclusion, the way that one feels virtuous for walking a mile in the cold rain. We sing without our throats, hoarse from talking into the wind.

Feather upon feather and everything compels this sugar; the hand swings wider. If I could rake the snake out of those birds, they might finally stop singing? The Witch says: Give me another pair of children, and I'll give you a potion for eternal salvation.

Alternate middle #43

G. and H. let the Witch's house burn, run out of the house, grabbing a few hot gumdrops on the way out, and keep running until they get back to their Father's house, which they immediately set on fire. One taste of vengeance may lead to another.

The Monster's tools may undo the Master's house.

or

The Mother's tools may unmake the Father's house.

As you wish.

The widowed Father runs out of the burning cottage and is shocked to see his two children very much alive: dirty and smelly, faces and limbs covered in soot, and strangely unhappy, arms crossed over their rigid frames. H. looks almost fat; G. terribly thin. H. holds his Father's axe, the one that Father had strung up in a tree to make the children think he was chopping wood just a little ways away.

"What have you done?" cries the Father.

"We decided to come back," says G.

"Not what you expected?" says H.

"We'll let you live," says G. "But you'll have to start over."

"Where's Mother?" asks H.

"Dead," says Father, looking sad.

"Starvation, I presume," says G. dryly.

"Stroke," says the Father. "She was so young."

"We're younger," says H.

"We'll let you start over alone then," says G.

"Goodbye," says H.

"You selfish, terrible children," says the Father.

"We just did you a favor," says G. "Be grateful."

"Two," says H. "We survived and let you live. You have a chance now."

"Start over alone," says G. "It's your only way out of the Enchanted Woods."

"And this time, you'll get your first wish," says H. "We won't be coming back."

Two children, around the age of eight,

were found at the edge of the Enchanted Woods early this morning at 4:52 a.m. PDT. Forest Ranger P. Charming reported that she found the two children sleeping under a tree next to the Ranger's Lookout Station, as she was making her morning sweep of the area.

Ranger Charming noted that when she woke the children, who had been sleeping soundly in spite of the cold morning fog and cacophony of birdsong, they had looked frightened, the girl yelling, "Stay away from us!" and the boy suddenly wielding an axe that he'd apparently been sleeping on.

According to her report, Ranger Charming assured the children that she meant them no harm and asked them if they wanted to go inside the station, where it was warm and there was hot porridge and cocoa. The children, much to the Ranger's surprise, refused though they were clearly malnourished and seemed to have no provisions. The girl looked particularly thin.

"Inside is bad," said the boy.

"We don't want your candy," said the girl.

And with that the children bolted off back into the Enchanted Woods. Ranger Charming reported that she was unfortunately unable to catch up to the fleeing urchins, who as it turns out, may have been involved in two cottage fires that occurred earlier in the week, one, according to the police report, an act of arson by the homeowner's own children.

Another cottage

On the inside: walls made of metal painted white, and once inside there is no door, no windows. The children wish badly for the candy house or even their Father's cottage. G. takes the axe and begins hacking at a wall to no avail. H. takes the axe and tests the walls in different spots, tapping to see if any place sounds different. The metal walls ring and ring; they are hollow and seemingly impenetrable. The axe is their only tool, and none of this was apparent from the outside.

From the outside, the cottage had looked simple, clean, and ordinary—a bit friendly with a pot of blue and red flowers on the stone steps leading to the wooden door, which was embossed with the phrase

Velkommen. Mi casa es su casa.

Hungry again and reading neither language, the children entered preparing to do battle with whatever monster they found in there. Instead of a Witch or Other Aberration, they found an empty room, cool and soulless, the front door disappearing into the wall behind them. For the first time in their trials, H. and G. cry like children.

Their tears mix with the dirt and soot still covering their faces, and their crying leaves inky droplets on the spotless white floor. H. wipes his face, snuffling, and notices small holes in the floor where his tears have fallen.

"Look!" he says to G. "We must cry harder."

H. and G. huddle together and aim their faces at the floor and cry and cry and cry, making a small puddle, which becomes a hole that widens as their tears pour into it. They cry and cry until the hole is big enough for the children to see what's beneath the house, and what they see is water moving swiftly, the house on pillars six feet or so above the moving stream.

The children cry until the hole is big enough for them to fit through it. G. holds the axe with one hand and holds H.'s hand in the other as he lowers himself into the hole, his feet skimming the rapidly moving water. He can see the bottom of the house, which appears to be made of wooden beams.

G. quickly follows, hanging the blade of the axe on the edge of the hole and lowering herself down. H. is fully in the water, as G. lets go of the axe, which she cannot unlatch.

H. and G. are carried by the swift moving river past the edge of the cottage, which appears again to be made of stone and timber like any other house, back into the Woods where it is now dark, the great trees green-black around them. The river, which is quite wide, carries them faster and faster toward something, their destination of course unknown. The current is too swift and direct for the children to swim out of it to the shore.

Though the water is cool, G. does not feel cold. It is mildly pleasant to be in the stream, which is salty unlike any water she has felt or seen. The river continues to carry the children along as the moon and stars rise in the sky, the moon illuminating the whispering leaves along the riverbank. The children buoy easily in the salty water and eventually fall asleep.

When they awake with the light of day, H. and G. find themselves in a pool surrounded on three sides by steep, pine-covered mountains. A small waterfall drums into the pool. The children swim to the water's edge and sit looking at the gray-blue water and the falls.

"Where are we?" asks H.

"Lost," says G. "But this place looks better than the last."

No more sugar pills, oh glory, glory on high

Once upon a time, there was a little girl who had survived a great trial through remarkable grit, force, luck, and ruthless decisiveness. She knew that what had happened to her was quite terrible, but she would not know just how awful it was until many years later when she was a young adult with a larger consciousness and experience of the world to tell her that:

(1) Not everyone is tossed out into the Woods to fend for themselves.
(2) Most kids don't contend with being eaten by strangers.

However, she was also later not surprised to learn that these things did happen to some people and that much worse things happened to others—parents who chopped up their children and fed them to the other parent as strangely delicious stew, etc. So, as a young adult, this woman experienced first an intensifying of the outrage, fear, and betrayal she had felt as a child whose job it is to survive until he or she can leave the cottage for good.

As an adult, she saw many re-creations of this same story—abandonment, egregious violation of rights, attempted violations of person, resorting to violence to fend off violence, and finally, being told to act as if nothing unusual had happened. As a child and as an adolescent, it was the lying that rankled her most of all. She could not forgive her Father, because he refused, adamantly and psychotically, to admit to any wrongdoing. He was guiltless in his own conscience, considering himself a victim of stronger persons—his wives, the Witch. "Everybody saves themselves," he said. "I had no choice."

"It was you or I," said G. "That's the tragedy, that you see it that way always."

"You can't forgive anyone if you feel they've diminished you rather than set you upon your true path," said a wise woman, who had seen every worst imaginable thing.

What was the true path? thought G. All this wandering?

Which brings us to the ending or the other downside:

I can believe that H. returns to the Father's cottage but not G. I believe that those twins learned different lessons in those Woods, on that journey to the candy house of plenty and transparent duplicity. Like any two persons, they experienced the same events differently, and as you may recall, the events they experienced were also different. H., you'll remember, was being fattened up, while G. was given little to eat and was treated like a servant and a nuisance. G. had not been appeased, because the Witch had calculated that she did not need to be or perhaps she just liked the taste of boys better. In any case, this discrepancy in treatment may have been what did the Witch in; had she fed both of them, the girl too may have been so drunk on endorphins, so grateful to be fed that the Witch would have succeeded in her plan and had not one but two delectable children to eat. But as the story shows, you can't give a girl nothing, treat her like a slave, and expect her to suck it up forever, especially if that little girl has been starved before, and her brother is eating.

Which brings us to the beginning, as the ending seems so implausible for at least one of the protagonists. Even if the Stepmother had died while the children were scrambling through the dark, it's extremely unlikely that the Father, the Blood-Parent, the one who set up the axe as a decoy and led the children into the Woods twice, would have had a change of heart. He was still a poor Woodcutter. There would still not be enough to eat.

The tragedy of the story is that only one twin would know this, and hardship would have pushed those two apart, to be orphaned for a third time. H. had always wanted to go home: leaving those clever trails stone by stone, crumb by crumb. He expected to be fed eventually, and even the

Witch, the lowest caste of creature in the Woods, had fed him. G. may have tried to persuade him to try another path, one out of the Enchanted Woods, but H. wanted badly to believe that his Father loved him, that the person in charge approved of him, that it was only temporary insanity that had made him pack his children off into the forest.

The Stepmother, like the Witch, was dead. Perhaps the Stepmother was the Witch, disguising herself and setting a trap to finish the task that her husband wouldn't commit to. Those children, after all, had come back once already. Maybe all adult females were bad. In the patriarchal fantasy of the standard happy ending, we're left with a poor man twice widowed and his two grateful children living ever after on food and love that wasn't there to begin with. The tragedy is that only one of us sees it that way.

A FRESH WAY IN IS A FRESH WAY OUT

one

1. The roar of the wind through invisible leaves.
2. The sound of dirt beneath my feet.
3. Things a child wouldn't normally see.
4. How normal is this situation? We're all cast out sooner or later.
5. Mad at H. for packing crumbs this time.
6. Mad at myself for packing nothing.
7. Full stop.

two

1. The sound of cataracts running like money.
2. Cataract of the mountain, not the body.
3. We write the cruel stories to avoid them in our future lives.
4. To start down the path again, into the Woods with the birds and the thoughts as companions.
5. Dry as a chicken bone, narrow as a cane.
6. Stepmother—the blankest character, perhaps unfairly blamed.
7. What would a happy ending look like if not some form of home, companionship, domesticity?

three

1. Dot the margin, make it spread like butter.
2. The Woods were barren but safe.
3. Clever G., what will you do with the middle of the story?
4. The Witch's spectacular death was just the beginning.
5. Two women die. One man survives.

6. Always blame the other parent.
7. A particularly specious ending, improbable even for the genre.

four

1. A beautiful chocolate plum cake.
2. A blackbird rising from the steel-gray Sea.
3. Everyone can think of seven reasons to end it now or keep going.
4. What happened to the Blood-Mother?
5. The virtue of the ending lies in what does not happen: no Prince or Huntsman to the rescue, no pernicious dream-seeding of wishful thinking.
6. Hard as candy.
7. How was there suddenly enough?

five

1. *Mon dieu*, we'll be sick of this story.
2. We already are.
3. This tale should make you feel a little sick.
4. Crisped Witch.
5. A normal person wouldn't do this.
6. The sound of money and the afterlife.
7. Alternate ending #23: G. buries the Witch's ashes and stays in the candy house, which magically renews itself. The children forage mushrooms, berries, onions, and apples growing in the Woods. H. learns how to fish. They eat well. They go to school.

six

1. Alternate beginning #49: The Father tells them straight up, "I love you but not enough to save you. It *was* your Stepmother's idea, but I fully endorse it because I am weak,

and frankly my life and my marriage are more important than the two of you."

2. H. doesn't bother with the crumbs—one disappointment averted.
3. When they come upon the Witch's house, the children know full well that it may be a trap. A beautiful house made of candy is, of course, a little too good to be true. They eat it anyway given the lack of alternatives.
4. What if the house were made of gluten-free bread? Or something that the children *should* have been eating? Would that have been any better? Would it still be the Witch's house?
5. Good German chocolate, hazelnuts, marzipan lattice.
6. No matter the denouement for each protagonist, hunger is a constant. They will never get over being told that there wasn't enough.
7. However, knowing what they know, they don't go back to the Father's cottage. They forge on through the forest, eventually crossing into the Unenchanted Woods, where not surprisingly they continue to fend for themselves, which is an exquisite nuisance. However, in the wider World, there are benevolent adults—unlike the trio in the Woods of childhood.

seven

1. One is always at the mercy of bigger, stronger persons with greater access to the necessary resources: food, shelter, warmth, candy.
2. One is also always at the mercy of one's own hunger, which given a deep enough sense of deprivation will become greed, heedless. The children devouring the Witch's home, her art.

3. I would like to tell the tale so that it no longer makes me sad.
4. The Europeans ask, "But is the crisis apparent? Do you feel it?"
5. Having children can make you.
6. Like the Sea, dark with waves.
7. Alternate ending #5: The candy house catches on fire—all that burning sugar—and everyone goes down: the Witch, H., and G. The parents read about it in the paper and carry on with their strained, bewildered lives.

eight

1. The candy house catches on fire—all that burning fat—but the children run out, running from horror for the rest of their lives.
2. G. lives out of a suitcase for years in her adult life, a vagabond, barely unhomeless. Homeless.
3. She'll never understand how the Witch existed.
4. She'll never understand the desperation that would propel a Blood-Father to cast his children into surefire peril.
5. When he was 15, my Brother drove himself and the family car into a wall. He was living with my parents, whom we were both supporting, because they didn't have enough.
6. Our Blood-Mother went to the hospital, eyes full of self-pity, and asked my Brother for the rent money.
7. She blamed her actions on our Father.

nine

1. My Father could have gotten a job, which he eventually did.
2. The solution turned out to be very simple.
3. My Brother forgave them.
4. I did not.
5. I couldn't fathom acting on that fear, knowing it myself.

6. Alternate ending #1: I did not love them enough.
7. Forgiveness is the hardest luck.

ten

1. Do I feel bad? Of course. That's why I'm writing this terrible story.
2. It's raining, and the rain is incredibly lovely.
3. Those stones in H.'s pockets were dead weight, the way back proving useless.
4. You can choose a lighter path, go through that door with nothing on your person, nothing on your back.
5. And keep going, through door after door of each successive room in each successive house until you find the one that's just right, not the tragic illogic of the cottage of youth or the delusional candy house, but the one that fits, made of wood, stone, mortar, and brick.
6. To make lists is to privilege control and order above all else, to love elegance, sparseness, and the idea of progression, way giving onto way.
7. Some endings cannot be rewritten, and that's alright. The ones who did the damage must want to be forgiven. In the meantime, put down the stone that wishes for rescue. Step through door after door without looking back. Be in the new strange. As a wise man said, it's easier than you think.

III

. . . THE PAGES TURNING. THE BLUE PINAFORE. WHITE SLEEVES, RED CHERUB CHEEKS FLUNG INTO THE UNKNOWN . . . WHAT IS THE CRUMB/DIAMOND OF THIS STORY?

you could have been R. in her blood-red glamour bursting intrepid from the Wolf's lower mouth or C. in her tight shoes and pail full of dust.

you are G. as straw fence, pile of wood, pile of stones, yellow flower.

you are G. as sun on iron, G. as would-be ballad, as would-be balladeer.

you are G. as wooden shutters, inferior first-floor view.

you are G. as green border on thin straw mat.

you are G. sick of the high road.

you are G. as clenched jaw that won't unpin.

you are G. as temporary subject, temporary friend.

you are G. with a tepid hangover that should be worse.

you are G. writing a novel about patricidal hatred, inherited misogyny, and looking for good kin.

you are G. as little Korean American Fräulein . . .

In the fantastical world we are watching,

the Black women are victims, the White women are sluts, the Black men are violent monsters, the White men are brave heroes, and the Asian men are inconsequential. We are watching this world as it flickers against a bare, white wall, and we think it lacks imagination, as it resembles several of the made-up worlds we've already watched. The characters speak clearly and smoothly in the world we are watching. There are young and old White males, and they are nice to each other.

This fantastical world flickers and hums before our eyes, expanding from a blue beam of light. This world was made by a famous Believer, a man with a graying beard who lives across the river in the far North. We would like to know why the Believer of this world made the Black men so violent and ill-tempered. When the White people break the law in this land, which is covered with hills and trees like ours, it is to help orphans. They want to give the orphans a house to live in, food, names, education, and useful skills. In this Believer's world, when the Black men break the law of this land, they do it to hurt their own children, raping them.

We are orphans, but we do not understand this made-up world or how the orphans live together like the dwarves or the bears. We have never lived in a big house with other orphans or met any other orphans in all our travels. We live in the Woods by ourselves. Sometimes we take shelter in a cave or a clearly unoccupied building, if it looks ordinary. We no longer trust fancy houses that look like our childhood fantasies. The first thing we do when we enter a house is figure out how to quickly escape, should a Witch or a tired, hungry bear or an adult show up.

We have also never met a Black, Asian, or Latinx man or woman in the woods. We have met many White men with knives, such as the Huntsman and the Fowler. Our Father had axes because he is a Woodsman. We took one of the axes for protection, but we lost it when we went into a hole in the floor to escape the house with the unbreakable white metal walls. The axe got stuck on the edge of the hole, which closed itself around the axe after we dropped down into the River of Children's Tears and floated away.

In our world, the women, who are White, are monsters not sluts. A monster is someone who wants to eat, kill, or have sexual relations with children. We know about the first two, though we prevented those things from happening.

That was our happy ending: inhibition. This is our denouement: wandering and growing.

Someday we will be adults, bigger than our Father and dead Stepmother. Bigger than the Witch, who was not so large physically. We do not know if the Witch counts as a woman. We call her "she" and "her," because it is convenient.

We do not know if our real Mother was a victim, as she died right after giving birth to us. Our Stepmother may too have been a victim. Our Father said it was a stroke, but our Father has been known to bend the truth. Our Father is also a monster if you count aiding and abetting the abandonment and inevitable demise of your own children as depraved. He blamed it on our Stepmother, but she cannot speak for herself. In our world, most people view him with pity and indifference, though that is also how they treat everybody. It is OK to be a monster if you live by yourself.

In our world, the heroes are children, so we are not too excited about becoming adults, though it will be good to have all the food.

When we are adults, we will build an ordinary-looking house with seven good escape routes, and we will let only orphans into the house. We will build a strong door, and we will get another axe.

When we watch the other made-up worlds, we do not know which real and fantastical worlds they correspond to. There are so many Believers and so many worlds coming out of the Believers' hands and mouths.

Sometimes we have found ourselves outside the Enchanted Woods, transported by the wind, a river, or our feet to another land. Sometimes we just watch the other worlds and spend a little time in them to think upon their strangeness with mixtures of confusion, rage, helplessness, and admiration.

Having successfully avoided Three Unsavory Fates—

being married to a bully, being married to a passive-aggressive post-feminist, being married to a feckless charmer—G. found herself free as the birds who ate H.'s crumbs, free and, of course, alone.

"Free to be alone anywhere though," thought G. Meaning: free to change the backdrop, and changing the backdrop can change the inside out.

> "The art of leaving isn't hard to master,
> leave it harder, leave it last or
> first or whatever . . ."

G. gleefully mangled the poet's sad, witty verse, repurposing the poem.

In avoiding three disasters, G. had, of course, embraced another, that of the solitary wanderer—like Odysseus, unable to stay put long enough to enjoy the incredibly well-defended fruits of hearth and home even after being away and sowing all kinds of magical oats for 20 years. Especially after 20 years.

Crossing that threshold back to civilization, the land of routine and domesticity, slaying the old frenemies yucking it up in *your* house, pursuing *your* spouse, disguising yourself as a beggar—that part was fun, and shooting down those guys one by one, that part was easy, a continuation of the Action! Bringing that adventure back into the old domicile . . . it's staying that's hard. Abundance and logic can cure everything but hunger and the drive to drown it or kill it.

G. IS NOT G. BUT A SNAKE OF HERSELF IN HER OWN GARDEN.

She feels very far away from everyone she loves and claims to love in her own heart. Her neck and shoulders are a mess. It is another beautiful day in Paradise, a paradise like a Hell of her own making. She is surprised by her irritability, though she is not surprised by her aggravation with the lack of privacy in Paradise, the lack of neutrality, which is the state she craves.

Everyone is irritable. Everyone hates everyone else in Paradise. G. knows that the Woolgatherer is writing unruffled, articulate stories about their interactions, how their pleasantries are belied by resentment or some such nonsense. G. dislikes realistic fiction very much.

LA CHINITA IS WALKING DOWN THE RED BRICK PATH,

down the hill, listening to El Rubio prattle on about his French mother, who has been dead for four years. El Rubio is red-haired not blond; La Chinita is Korean not Chinese; both are American. El Rubio talks about how he was his mother's favorite and thus his older sisters hated him.

"I almost hate him," thinks La Chinita, "and I just met him. He never stops talking, and he's clearly obsessed with his mother even though he's almost 50." She thinks that it's not a coincidence that he's spent his romantic life alone in spite of storybook good looks, a successful career, money, and sociability. She thinks about women hobbling their sons with too much love, sending them boxes of homemade cookies on their 34th birthdays while they're completing their neurosurgery residencies or economics PhDs.

She is fervently jealous of that box of cookies, being treated like an infant, and how certain men through the influence of their uninterrupted need manage to make even that ridiculous behavior enticing. They will always be rescued, doted upon, sent jars of lingonberry jam, returning the favor with resentment and adoration for the all-powerful, all-serving Mother and her analogues whom they find and make.

Later in the day, when the hot sun beats through the breeze, she hears El Rubio crossing the courtyard, talking aloud to no one but himself.

Over the Sea

"There's a lot and a little both here," said the new Hansel, describing the small village G. had just arrived in. She had travelled to this village in the North at the invitation of K., the Director of an artists' residency in the village. G. had never heard of the place before, but she knew the area from the wanderings of her youth, as she had worked there among the fjords and mountains for one golden summer, picking red berries and preparing apples for the harvest. Unemployed now, she had truly had no money then, and all her possessions had fit into a green rucksack with leather straps, all her possessions being some clothes, toiletries, a laundry line, a sink plug, and some books including a biography of Gandhi, which a kind man in the South had given her and which she still hadn't read.

That was the first time she'd left the cottage, leaving H. behind to fend for himself, as there had been no persuading him to leave.

"I'm more dependent," he had said. "I'm the baby." He was younger by only a few minutes, but G. had understood this statement to be mostly true. So she'd packed her rucksack and found out where she could take a ship across the Sea to P________, the furthest place she could think of. She already knew her way around and through the Woods by heart and had figured it would take two days travel on foot to get out of the forest and to the harbor where the ship was. She had left the cottage in the very early morning before anyone else was up, leaving a note on the breadbox that said, "I won't be returning this time. Please give H. my share of the food. —G." Then she had added: "And remember: There's always *enough*."

Even then—especially then—G. had felt rage and distrust for her Stepmother and contemptuous pity for her Father's weakness and the way he caved over and over again to their Stepmother's attempts to starve, eject, and passively kill H. and G., in spite of telling them how much he cared for them. G. distinctly remembered the look on his face when they had returned to the cottage—dirty, exhausted, and tick-ridden, H. still plump from the Witch's nefarious overfeeding, G. scraggly as a chicken foot. Their Father had smiled before crying out and embracing them, but for an instant before that, there was a flash of something else, fear perhaps or what G. later interpreted as self-pity for the struggles to come.

The escape, therefore, had been easy. No one had stopped her, as G. had known no one would, and no one came looking for her. She had slipped through the forest along a familiar series of paths, leaving the Enchanted Woods and making her way to the seaside port where she would begin the voyage.

And that had been a fantastic summer, beginning with that first journey across the dark blue ocean. Prior to setting out, G. had earned a little bit of money by doing chores for an elderly couple who had taken pity on her and H., and she worked on board the ship, scrubbing the latrines and washing the deck each night to pay for her fare. The work was so easy; she left the latrines and deck gleaming. She had always worked, and the ship's crew supervisor was pleased with her efforts, which did and did not surprise her.

In the months and years to come, G. would do many jobs that would satisfy many bosses in different lands: picking oranges in the South, serving beer to the pale men and women in L________, gathering signatures for the population counts in R______, selling books of mostly low value in the big city of B________, and of course more cleaning and carting and lifting.

All that was decades ago, thought G., who now in middle age, had found herself for the first time, suddenly unemployed.

And here was a new Hansel, who looked nothing at all like the old one who, like G., had pitch-black hair with eyes to match. The new H. was large with dirty blond hair and goofy blue eyes like the storybook Hansels that

G. had read about. He wore a striped black-and-white shirt, as if he'd just gotten out of a comic book jail, and had a small paunch and a very direct gaze. As it turned out, the new H. was exactly G.'s age.

G. didn't know what her Brother looked like anymore, though she imagined him to still be a bit chubby, perhaps bearded and rabbinical but more Asiatic. G.'s own weight had waxed and waned throughout her adulthood according to her financial station. The poorer she was, the more she ate, ever since she had had the means to feed herself. And during her bouts of wanderlust, when she absolutely could not stay in one place for more than a few weeks at a time—there had been four thus far—she either put on the pounds from anxiety and inertia or shed them from overactivity and illness.

This time she was ravenous, eating bowl after bowl of muesli with the sour cultured milk of this Northern land, fried sausages, salads of beets and hard-boiled eggs, tubes of cod roe dyed bright pink, thick slices of brown bread with butter, triple helpings of noodles with tomatoes or butter. The Witch would have been very pleased.

New Hansel was sitting across from G. at a long wooden table. G. offered him a tube of mayonnaise and somewhat reluctantly pushed a box of half-eaten oat crackers toward him, asking, "Do you want these?" Clearly somewhat disgusted, he declined, which made G. smile with relief.

Wolf across the hall

It was another 30 years before G. felt that very few people wanted to eat her or do her monstrous harm. Most people, she concluded, had enough of a handle on themselves to be indifferent, and only a few were wired to commit murder, cannibalism, child sacrifice. Most of us, thought G., bury that stuff or don't feel it. Who knows what the others really think? Not I, thought G.

Alternate ending #3

Bare bones, bare bones, the Witch's bones charred and cracked in the black iron oven, all that was left of her when we went back there some weeks after we burned our Father's house. We did not return intentionally but by accident, stumbling upon the gooey remains of the Witch's house in our wanderings. We were, it appeared, permanently lost, the Enchanted Woods shifting its paths day to day by an unpredictable design, so that we never knew where a familiar branch or path would lead. The shifting of the paths began after we left our Father's house, which we had had no trouble finding.

Coming into a circular clearing, we recognized immediately the remains of the candy house by the odor of burned flesh that lingered, mixed with the delectable smell of burnt candy, which still drew us in and which had melted and coagulated to a hard, sticky pool spreading from the oven like the old floor of the house.

A cold needling rain was steadily pelting the candy floor, the oven, us, and the trees around the clearing, with their charred and miraculously still green leaves. The fire had not extended further than the grounds of the house due to either the enchantment of the Woods or the Witch's intent. She may have cast a protective net around her magical house, of which nothing but the oven, two cauldrons, and the candy floor were left.

The house had burned. The Witch was dead. Those were her bones blackened and hissing in the cooling oven, which was still warm to the touch. Yet, still we sensed we might feel her bony fingers tap our shoulders or grab our wrists at any minute. Or that we might turn around and see her hovering above us with her craggy face, her large incisors, and light-colored hair blowing behind her. We expected her to appear and yell at us for trespassing, for disturbing her peace.

She was dead—we had shoved her in the oven ourselves—but she did not feel dead. We had pushed her in with our own hands, sealing the iron door shut as she thrashed and cursed us, wishing us short, unhappy lives, a redundant wish. G. had pressed her hands against the oven door and had the burned palms to prove it.

We did not know what spell the Witch had cast to make us feel that things were not over when they were or how she made us think of her existence and death when we did not want to think of any hideous, unpleasant things. The Woods had treated us well for the most part. We had found plenty to eat in the forest and shelter when we needed it. Most of the animals did not try to eat us, and we fended off those that did with much less effort than it took to kill the Witch or leave our Father for good. Our hearts' desire was to never think of the Witch again, to never feel her threats as real, and to leave the Enchanted Woods. But we found ourselves often thinking about the Witch and our Father, and we could not find our way out of the forest.

Using the axe and the shovel we had found in the Huntsman's shed, we carved a pit in the candy floor, cracking the hard surface and digging and digging down through the moist black dirt. Using the shovel, we removed the bones from the oven and threw them into the pit, putting all the ashes in as well. We covered the hole with dirt and fresh leaves and recited the following words:

> You tried to kill us and eat us
> and now you're dead.
> Because you're dead,
> we say
> goodbye.
> You can't be angry or hungry

anymore.
There's no need.
No need.
So, goodbye.

As we were digging, burying the bones, and saying the words, the rest of the candy floor melted away in the rain, leaving a square of beautiful wet dirt, which we walked across to head into the Woods again. At the edge of the clearing, we heard a loud soughing noise and turned to see the oven sinking into the earth, sucked down as if by a great tunnel of wind. The axe also flew out of H.'s hand and into the tunnel, and we feared we might be sucked in as well, but then the hole suddenly closed over. We noticed small shoots of grass and weeds pop up where the candy house had been. We re-entered the Woods having witnessed some magic at last.

And through the Woods

The next door was always around the corner leading to a new realm where the natives are kind to strangers, and apples grow on trees like so much money. Where the average citizen lives to be 98, and even the lame wheel freely down the paths through the Woods. Where the response to tragedy is not hysteria but sadness, and where the young, strong Huntsmen kill an elk or a moose each summer just prior to the Equinox and share the bounty with everyone in the village so that those who are too old or too weak to hunt may eat as well.

"You think that such a place does not exist, but I will tell you that it does," said G. "I lived there in my youth and a quarter century later, and this place, unlike the others I revisited, was virtually unchanged."

Like Sleeping Beauty in her castle of thorns, but richer upon awakening.

But what price, you ask, because everything comes with a price, you say, not believing that some imaginary and real worlds are better than others.

"The same price as always," acknowledged G. "Loneliness and the permanence of loss, which I can tell you is the only thing we ever have, as it is the only thing that lasts, and here," she added, "they feel it unadorned, without distraction, having no poverty, no crime, enough food and work for everyone. Their grief is felt keenly, and some do die of it. Their divorce rate is the same as yours. Abundance and logic can cure everything but heartache and the drive to drown it or kill it."

DREAM SONG 523 / G.

"I want to show you the view from under the bed," said the man with the sandy, silvering hair. He was a handsome man around my age—I knew this though I could not see his face. I had taken the elevator to the fifth floor in order to reach the fourth floor, though I had started on the second. This is how it worked: you had to go up to go down, and each floor was quite tall, the equivalent of several stories. I met the man and his dogs on my way back down, somewhere between the fifth and fourth floors. I don't recall the elevator doors opening, but there we were inside a dark green forest overhung with enormous leaves, along with his amiable dogs, one of which was golden with an absurdly elongated torso, a strange version of a retriever, who looked directly at me, grinned and walked off.

I knew I could trust this man; he seemed so inherently kind, so trustworthy, a man I'd been seeking: a guide, a shaman-husband. "The view from *under* the bed," he said, as we approached his cottage, and it occurred to me that perhaps I should not be so trusting—the proposition seemed both sexual and not. Would we do it under the bed? I hoped so! Maybe I could corner him under there, but then maybe I would die of embarrassment if his intentions turned out to be pure. This man, whose face I could not see, whom I wanted to trust so badly. He seemed like a reliable person, but how good could the view from under the bed be? I thought of my own bed, which I checked under every night before going to sleep, along with the closets and the shower stall, and how the view would be either of a blank wall, some cobwebs, or the floor of my plain, rather monastic room. Had he dropped some change down there? Was there hidden treasure behind the wall? Was that what he was trying to tell me? Or was he an excellent liar like me, impersonating kindness and trying to kill me?

Under the bed means under sex, under sleep, under the place of dreams and illness and recovery and frailty, under comfort, under pain, under isolation, and under union—the foundation below the body in its mostly unknown and most vulnerable positions.

"I want to show you the spirit level," he could have said if he hadn't been so opaque, but I appreciated his implied argument that the spirit is lower than the body and more ordinary, that it looks like nothing at all, like the worn rug you step on every day, like dead insects and dust and loose hair on the floor.

Acknowledgments

I would like to thank the editors Liz Powell, Jessica Hendry Nelson, Jensen Beach, Harilaos Stecopoulos, Lynne Nugent, Jenna Hammerich, Nick Twemlow, Krystal Languell, Rebecca Wolff, Jess Puglisi, Jason Zuzga, Seth Luke, Ariel Resnikoff, Orchid Tierney, Christian Peet, Resh Daily, Meg Forjater, and everyone else at the following publications where excerpts of *H & G* previously appeared: *The Iowa Review*, *Pamplemousse*, *Bone Bouquet*, *Fence*, *Green Mountains Review*, *JuxtaProse*, *Supplement*, and *Tarpaulin Sky Magazine*. Special thanks also to the editors and readers at Tarpaulin Sky Press for selecting *H & G* as a finalist for the 2017 Tarpaulin Sky Book Prizes.

Many thanks to Fundación Valparaíso and Kunstnarhuset Messen for granting me residencies where much of this work was composed, with special thanks to Ingunn van Etten for granting me an extended stay at the latter in the fjordlands of Western Norway.

Much gratitude also to the Corporation of Yaddo for giving me time and glorious space to revise the manuscript and to read the work-in-progress to an ideal audience of writers, composers, and artists. I am also deeply grateful to Ursinus College for supporting the revision and submission of this work, and to Prageeta Sharma and Joanna Klink, founders and producers of the Thinking Its Presence: Race & Creative Writing Conference at the University of Montana, where I read early versions of the novella to other excellent audiences of writers and scholars.

Thank you to Darlene Chandler Bassett, Tracey Cravens-Gras, Alex Martin, and everyone at the A Room of Her Own Foundation for supporting the novella's award of the inaugural Clarissa Dalloway Prize and for your vital encouragement of women writers. I am proud to be associated with Virginia Woolf's legacy and vision.

I am indebted to Julia Bloch and Rachel Zolf for suggesting that I send *H & G* to Sidebrow Books and to David Micah Greenberg, Joanna Klink, James Hannaham, David Groff, Michael Snediker, Rachel Levitsky, John Keene, and Rosa Alcalá for crucial advice regarding the book's publication.

A million thank you's too to Jason Snyder, Kristine Leja, and John Cleary at Sidebrow for embracing this project and for all that you do on behalf of iconoclastic writing. It's been a true pleasure to work with you throughout the editorial process and an honor to be in the company of Sidebrow's other authors.

And all my love and gratitude to friends here and abroad who provided me with sustenance—literal, aesthetic, and spiritual homes—during the writing of this book including: Phil Pardi, Carolyn Mow, and Emilio Mow Pardi, Jackie Haught and Phyllis Bloom, Perry Sayles and Steve Harvey, Pam Thurschwell and Jim Endersby, Sarah Goldfine-Ward, Mark and Karen Howenstein, Daphne Brooks, Mireille Roddier, Laetitia Coussement, Agathe Simon, Mario D'Souza and Philippe Gilbert, Christopher Wendell Jones and Ann Yi, James Hannaham and Brendan Moroney, Nick Turse, Ann Jones, Irene Lusztig, Barbara Weinstein, Tony Nadler and Alice Leppert, Sally Carpenter, Kathryn Goettl, Elizabeth and Dennis Goettl, Katarina Burin and Matt Saunders, Sasha Rossman and Jan Dietrich, Amy Sillman, Taylor Davis and Sue Schardt, Elizabeth McQuitty and Arthur Lee, Annemor and Olav Jåstad, Ragnhild Jåstad Vågen and Kjell-Jostein Vågen, Ingeborg and Reinhardt Jåstad Røyset, Svein and Ingunn Jåstad, Kari Jaastad, and Gunnhild Jaastad.

Your generosity, friendship, and hospitality have meant the World to me.

Anna Maria Hong's first poetry collection, *Age of Glass*, won the Cleveland State University Poetry Center's 2017 First Book Poetry Competition and will be published in early 2018. Her second poetry collection, *Fablesque*, won Tupelo Press's Berkshire Prize and is forthcoming in 2019. A former Bunting Fellow at the Radcliffe Institute for Advanced Study, she has published fiction and poetry in over 50 journals and anthologies including *The Nation*, *The Iowa Review*, *Poetry*, *Ecotone*, *Mandorla*, *Green Mountains Review*, *Bennington Review*, *Conduit*, *Fence*, *Harvard Review*, *Southwest Review*, *The Volta*, and *The Best American Poetry*. She will join the Literature faculty at Bennington College in July 2018.

SIDEBROW BOOKS | www.sidebrow.net

ON WONDERLAND & WASTE
Sandy Florian
Collages by Alexis Anne Mackenzie
SB002 | ISBN: 0-9814975-1-9

BEYOND THIS POINT ARE MONSTERS
Roxanne Carter
SB009 | ISBN: 0-9814975-8-6

SELENOGRAPHY
Joshua Marie Wilkinson
Polaroids by Tim Rutili
SB003 | ISBN: 0-9814975-2-7

THE COURIER'S ARCHIVE & HYMNAL
Joshua Marie Wilkinson
SB010 | ISBN: 0-9814975-9-4

NONE OF THIS IS REAL
Miranda Mellis
SB005 | ISBN: 0-9814975-4-3

FOR ANOTHER WRITING BACK
Elaine Bleakney
SB011 | ISBN: 1-940090-00-8

LETTERS TO KELLY CLARKSON
Julia Bloch
SB007 | ISBN: 0-9814975-6-X

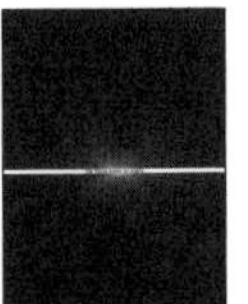

THE VOLTA BOOK OF POETS
A constellation of the most innovative poetry evolving today, featuring 50 poets of disparate backgrounds and traditions
SB012 | ISBN: 1-940090-01-6

SPED
Teresa K. Miller
SB008 | ISBN: 0-9814975-7-8

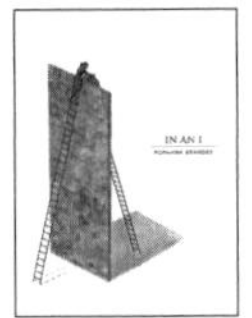

IN AN I
Popahna Brandes
SB013 | ISBN: 1-940090-02-4

VALLEY FEVER

Julia Bloch

SB014 | ISBN: 1-940090-03-2

THE YESTERDAY PROJECT

Ben Doller & Sandra Doller

SB015 | ISBN: 1-940090-04-0

THE WINE-DARK SEA

Mathias Svalina

SB016 | ISBN: 1-940090-05-9

FIELD GLASS

Joanna Howard & Joanna Ruocco

SB017 | ISBN: 1-940090-06-7

INHERIT

Ginger Ko

SB018 | ISBN: 1-940090-07-5